PETS FROM SPACE

COSMIC CLAWS

Jan Burchett and Sara Vogler

Illustrated by Alex Paterson

Orion
Children's Books

First published in Great Britain in 2014
by Orion Children's Books
a division of the Orion Publishing Group Ltd
Orion House
5 Upper St Martin's Lane
London WC2H 9EA
An Hachette UK company

1 3 5 7 9 10 8 6 4 2

ISBN 978 1 4440 1182 1

Printed in Great Britain by Clays Ltd, St Ives plc

www.orionbooks.co.uk

For Lenny Rusinek Graham

J.B. & S.V.

For Angus

A.P.

RENFREWSHIRE COUNCIL	
192565921	
Bertrams	15/07/2014
	£4.99
MOB2	

CONTENTS

Whizz! Bang! Crackle!

Tom Bright was in the garden.

His friends, Zack and Daisy, were helping him train his pet dog, Fizz.

Tom, Zack and Daisy knew that Fizz wasn't really a dog.

After all, dogs aren't usually purple with yellow spots.

And dogs don't have trumpet noses.

And dogs can't talk.

Fizz was just pretending to be a dog. He was really a Satnik from the planet Saturn. He was on a secret mission to investigate Earth and his spaceship was sitting at the bottom of Tom's pond. It had crash-landed there last week.

Well, splash-landed.

Tom, Zack and Daisy had an unusual class rabbit too. He was called Toppo.

Toppo wasn't really a rabbit.

Rabbits don't usually have zebra stripes.

And rabbits don't have corkscrew ears.

And rabbits can't talk.

Toppo was just pretending to be a rabbit. He was really a Satnik, like Fizz.

He'd popped out of the pond to investigate school – and to play some Top Toppo Tricks. Now, he lived in their classroom.

There were more Satniks still on the spaceship. Tom, Zack and Daisy couldn't wait to meet them. But they had to keep the Satniks a secret. They knew that grown-ups must never find out that aliens had landed on Earth. Grown-ups would be very silly about that kind of thing.

Unfortunately,
it wasn't easy keeping the
Satniks a secret. They didn't always behave
like Earth pets, so Tom was teaching Fizz
how to follow a scent like a dog.

Daisy was teaching him
how to beg like a dog.

And Zack was
teaching him how to
dig a hole like a dog.

Tom was just going to show Fizz how to play dead when he spotted something lying by the pond. It was blue and floppy and very wet.

"What's that?" he said. "It looks like a mop."

"Zoops!" squeaked the mop. "I'm not a mop. I'm Zingle."

Tom jumped in surprise. Mops didn't usually talk — well, apart from the one that had said "mind the puddle" to him once.

Two big round eyes appeared in the mop, then two antennae popped up and began waving about.

"You must be a Satnik!" exclaimed Tom.

"Of course I'm a Satnik, silly Earthling," squeaked Zingle.

Zack and Daisy ran over.

"Cosmic!" said Zack. "Another Satnik to investigate Earth!"

"Poor thing," said Daisy. "You're soaking wet!"

"Of course I am," squeaked Zingle. "I've just swum out of the spaceship." Zingle began to roll around the garden, squeaking loudly.

Tom was delighted. He hadn't met a rolling Satnik before.

"Is Zingle investigating?" he asked Fizz.

"No," said Fizz. "She's upset. She hates having wet fur."

"And my fur takes ages to dry," squeaked Zingle as she rolled past.

"The only thing that will help is a swooshblotter," said Fizz.

"What's a swooshblotter?" asked Daisy.

"I'll show you on my Satpad," said Fizz. He twisted his ear.

Ping!

A silver cube shot out, transformed itself into a tiny computer and landed on his hand. He poked the keys with his nose.

The image of a peculiar machine shimmered in the air.

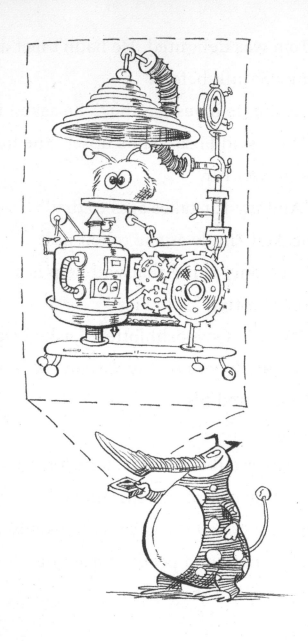

"I'll see if there's one in the shed,"
said Tom.

"There won't be," said Zack. "I don't
think there are any swooshblotters on
Earth."

"Oh, no!" squeaked Zingle as she
whizzed past. "My fur will never be dry
again."

"Every planet has swooshblotters,"
said Fizz. "I'll use my super Satpower to
find one. My super Satpower can find
anything." He poked the Satpad keys
again. "Just listen for the bleeps."

They listened.

"I can't hear any bleeps," said Daisy.

"Won't take long," said Fizz cheerfully.
"Any minute now."

"Hurry!" squeaked Zingle.

They listened again.

There were still no bleeps.

The Satpad folded itself into a cube and flew back into Fizz's ear.

"There aren't any swooshblotters on Earth," he announced.

Zingle rolled past at high speed, covering them in soggy pondweed.

"What do swooshblotters do?" asked Tom.

"They dry fur, of course," said Fizz.

"We've got things that dry fur," said Zack. "They're called hairdryers!"

"Zoops!" said Fizz. "They sound interesting. Will they work on Zingle?"

"Well, they work on baboons," said Daisy. "Baboons love them."

Daisy knew lots about animals.

Her dad was a keeper at The Really Wild
Wildlife Park.

"Wait there!" said Tom. "I'll get my

mum's hairdryer."

He raced towards
the house, skidded to
a halt and raced back.
"I forgot," he said.
"Mum said I mustn't
touch it any more."

"Was it when you
blew up those balloons to go to the
moon?" asked Zack.

"No," said Tom.

"Was it when you
borrowed it for juggling
practice?" asked Daisy.

"'Course not," said
Tom. "It was when
I used it to make a
snowstorm in my
bedroom."

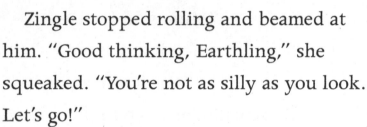

"Then we'll go to
my house," said Zack.
"We can use my sister's."

Zingle stopped rolling and beamed at
him. "Good thinking, Earthling," she
squeaked. "You're not as silly as you look.
Let's go!"

"But we must keep you hidden," said
Daisy.

"I've got just the thing," said Tom,
pulling a pair of his dad's underpants
off the washing line.

He wrapped Zingle up in them.

"This is fun!" came Zingle's muffled voice.

They were just setting off down the path when Tom's mum called them back.

Tom was horrified. Had Mum seen Zingle in Dad's underpants?

"Where are you going with Fizz?" she asked.

Tom breathed a sigh of relief. "To Zack's house," he said.

"You can't take him there!" said Mum. "He'll disturb Zack's gran. She's not been well."

"But he'll be ever so good," Tom begged.

"Zack's gran needs peace and quiet," said Mum firmly. "Fizz is staying here."

"Don't worry," Fizz whispered to Tom. "I'll show your mum how to dig a hole in the carpet."

Tom, Zack and Daisy set off down the road to Zack's house. Tom carried Zingle in Dad's underpants.

A woman stopped and peered at the bundle in Tom's arms. "Whatever have you got in those underpants?" she asked suspiciously.

"Er . . . it's a mop," said Tom.

"I'm not a mop!" squeaked Zingle.

"It doesn't sound like
a mop," said the woman.

Zingle's eyes peered out.

"And it doesn't look like a mop," said
the woman. "In fact, it's alive! Where did
you get it?"

"We found it," said Tom.

"On the grass," added Zack.

Zingle began to wriggle and squeak.

"Oh, dear," gasped the woman. "You
can't just pick things up like that. It could
be dangerous! There's only one thing to
do with dangerous things. I'm taking it
to the police."

Before Tom could stop her, the woman
snatched Dad's underpants and marched
off. Zingle began to squeak loudly in panic.

"We've got to stop that woman!"
cried Zack.

"But how can we?" asked Daisy.

"Let's catch her in a giant net,"
suggested Tom.

"We haven't got a giant net," said Zack.

"Then we'll zap her with a tranquilliser
dart," said Tom.

"We haven't got a tranquilliser dart either!" Daisy pointed out.

"I know what we'll do!" said Tom. "We'll make a sign saying *No talking mops wrapped in underpants allowed in here* and we'll run round and put it on the door of the police station before she arrives."

"We haven't got time for that!" exclaimed Zack.

"Good morning to you!" came a voice from a nearby bush.

A rabbit hopped out. Well, it wasn't really a rabbit. It had zebra stripes and corkscrew ears.

"Toppo!" exclaimed Daisy. "What are you doing so far from school?"

"I was just investigating that thing called glue when I heard Zingle

squeaking," said Toppo, "so I finished
sticking the piano to the wall bars,
jumped out of the stockroom window
and here I am."

They could hear Zingle's frantic
squeaks as the woman reached the corner.

"Time for a Top Toppo Trick," announced
Toppo.

"Cosmic!" said Tom. "I hope it's as good as the one with the book bag and the mashed potato."

"There's no time for tricks," said Daisy firmly. "Zingle needs rescuing!"

But Toppo was already twisting his ear.

Ping!

His Satpad popped out. He tapped the keys with a claw and waved it at the woman.

The woman began to float up into the air.

"Now she can't get away!" chuckled Toppo.

"But we can't get Zingle," said Daisy.

They raced to the corner.

"Help!" cried the woman as she hovered over a hedge. "What's happening?"

"We can't tell her it's an alien with a super Satpower," whispered Zack.

"Perhaps you've got bouncy shoes,"
Daisy called.

"Or springy socks," shouted Zack.

"Or you've eaten too many beans,"
yelled Tom.

The woman floated up to the top of
a lamp post. She gave a terrified cry,
clutched hold of the light and dropped
the underpants – with Zingle in them!

Daisy dived like a goalie and caught
the underpants in her arms.

Zingle was so surprised
she stopped squeaking.

"Follow me!" cried Zack.

They scampered into his garden and hid behind the gate.

"That was a top trick, Toppo," said Tom.

"But you'd better let the woman down now," said Daisy.

"Are you sure?" said Toppo, peering around the gatepost at her. "She looks very comfortable up there."

"Positive," said Zack.

Toppo waved his Satpad and the woman floated slowly down. She hit the ground and ran off screaming.

Toppo looked at Zingle.

"Zingle's got wet fur," he said in surprise.

"Come with us," said Tom. "We're going to dry her."

Toppo hopped into Tom's hood. "The only thing that will help is a swooshblotter," he said. "Have you got one?"

"Sort of," said Tom.

Zack pushed open his front door. He sniffed. "Dad's doing some baking!" he exclaimed.

"It smells better than plackernocks!" squeaked Zingle from the underpants.

"It even smells better than giggleblibs,"

said Toppo. "And I didn't think anything could smell better than giggleblibs."

Dad poked his nose around the kitchen door.

"Hello there," he said. "I'm making cupcakes. I'm hoping they might cheer Gran up. You lot can have some too when they're ready."

"Zoops!" said Toppo from Tom's hood.

Zack's dad looked at Tom, puzzled.

"Soup," said Tom quickly. "Very good for cheering grans up, but I'd much rather have cupcakes."

They made for the stairs.

"You'd better not go up there," said Zack's dad. "Gran's asleep in bed."

They tiptoed into the lounge. "Stay here," said Zack. "I'll get the hairdryer."

He rushed off. Soon he rushed back. "I can't find it!" he said.

"This is a disaster," squeaked Zingle.

She scrambled out of the underpants and shook pond water all over the carpet.

"I'll keep looking," said Zack desperately.

He rushed off again.

Zingle began to roll around the coffee table, squeaking in alarm.

"She'll wake up Zack's gran," said Tom. "We've got to stop her."

"I'll distract her," whispered Daisy. "It always works with pythons."

"Zack will be back soon, Zingle," called Daisy as Zingle whizzed up and down the curtains. "Why don't you practise being an Earth animal while you wait?"

Zingle stopped immediately and jumped down onto the sofa. "That's a good idea," she squeaked cheerfully. Then she frowned. "But I can't remember which animal I'm supposed to be."

"Have a look on your Satpad," said Tom. "Fizz wrote a list for Toppo so he'd know what to do when he came out of the spaceship. Perhaps he's written one for you."

Zingle twiddled her antennae.

Ping!

A Satpad flew out of her fur and landed on her paw. She tapped the keys.

A big list wobbled in the air.

"You're right, clever Earthling," she squeaked in surprise. "Fizz *has* written a list."

"Zoops!" squeaked Zingle. "I'm supposed to be a cat. I just have to grow long ears and say hee-haw!"

Zingle's Important List
by Fizz

1. Do not let Earthlings know you're an alien.
2. Except for Tom, Zack and Daisy.
3. Do not pretend to be a dog.
4. Do not pretend to be a rabbit.
5. Pretend to be a cat.
6. Make a cat nest.
7. Investigate Earth.

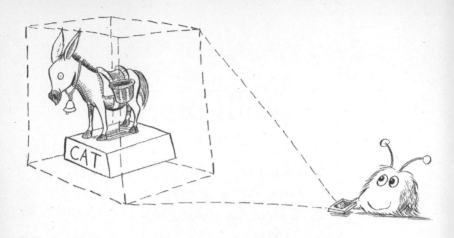

"That's not a cat," laughed Tom. "That's a donkey."

"Silly Earthling," squeaked Zingle. "It's a cat. Look!" She tapped the keys of the Satpad and an image shimmered in the air.

"That's definitely a donkey," said Daisy.

"Are you sure?" asked Zingle.

"Positive," said Daisy.

Zingle tapped the keys again. "Got it now," she squeaked.

She ran up the wall and hung upside down from the lampshade.

"That's not a cat either," laughed Tom. "That's a bat."

"What a relief," squeaked Zingle, plopping down. "I don't know how to fly." She gave her Satpad a shake. "All the animals are mixed up. The sprungles seem to be flobbered."

"Fizz and Toppo's Satpads are the same," said Daisy.

"It must have happened when the spaceship nearly hit Mars," squeaked Zingle. "Now I'll never find out how to be a cat."

"We can tell you that," said Tom. "Cats go miaow."

"Hee-haw!" squeaked Zingle cheerfully. "I mean miaow."

"And they purr when they're happy," said Daisy. "It's a sort of rumbling noise."

"And cats sit on laps," said Tom. "Now we have to decide whose pet you're going to be."

"That's easy!" squeaked Zingle, beaming. "I like this house. It smells nice. I'll live here with Zack."

"Great idea," said Tom.

The door burst open and Zack rushed in with a hairdryer.

"You lucky Earthling!" Zingle squeaked at him. "I'm going to be a cat and live with you. Where shall I make my cat nest?"

"Cosmic!" said Zack. "But cats don't make nests. We'll get you a nice basket."

"And cats hate getting their fur wet,

just like you, Zingle," said Daisy, "so let's get you dry."

"Hee-haw!" squeaked Zingle. "I mean miaow. About time!"

Zack plugged the hairdryer in. He switched it on.

There was a whirring sound, a puff of smoke and a very loud *BANG*!

Zack dropped the hairdryer and

pulled the plug out quickly.

"It's broken!"

he gasped.

"Broken?" squeaked Zingle.

Tom, Zack and Daisy put their fingers in their ears.

"What are you doing?" asked Zingle.

"We thought you were going to get upset again," said Tom.

"Of course I'm not, silly Earthlings," laughed Zingle.

She tapped the keys of her Satpad.

"This'll be fun," chuckled Toppo. "Zingle's going to use her super Satpower."

"What does it do?" asked Tom eagerly.

"You'll see," squeaked Zingle.

She aimed her Satpad at the hairdryer.

Whizz! Bang! Crackle!

A sparkling beam of light shot out. The hairdryer roared into life, dried Zingle's fur in an instant, and blew Toppo out of the window.

33

"Zingle's super Satpower fixes electrical things," Toppo called from the flowerbed.

"It certainly does," gasped Daisy.

"And it super-charges them!" yelled Tom in delight.

"Zoops!" squeaked Zingle. "It doesn't do that on Saturn. I'm going to use my super Satpower to investigate more electrical things."

She aimed her Satpad at the Hoover.

Whizz! Bang! Crackle!

The Hoover roared into life and chased Tom out of the door.

"That's interesting too," squeaked Zingle, running after him.

"We have to stop her," said Zack. "She'll wake up my gran!"

Zack and Daisy rushed into the hall.

Tom ran past, followed by the Hoover.

"You have to stop your investigations now, Zingle," Daisy told her.

"But I haven't finished yet, silly Earthling," squeaked Zingle. She aimed her Satpad into the kitchen.

Whizz! Bang! Crackle!

"Help!" came a cry from Zack's dad. "The food mixer's gone crazy!"

"That's *very* interesting!" squeaked Zingle.

"What's all this noise?" came a voice. Gran was riding slowly down the stairs on her stairlift.

Zingle aimed her beam at the stairlift.

"No!" shouted Zack in horror.

The stairlift shot to the bottom of the stairs.

"Faster!" yelled Gran as the stairlift shot up the stairs again.

"That's even more interesting," squeaked Zingle.

Zack's dad staggered into the hall. He was covered in egg and currants.

"It's a walking cake!" squeaked Zingle.

"It's not a walking cake," whispered Zack. "It's my dad."

"Are you sure?" asked Zingle.

"Positive!" whispered Zack. "And you've got to pretend to be a cat. Cats don't have super Satpowers."

Zingle tapped the keys on her Satpad.

Everything fell silent.

"Shame," said Gran as the stairlift came to a halt. "I was enjoying that."

"What happened?" gasped Zack's dad.

"Maybe the house got hit by lightning," said Zack.

"Or it was a power surge," said Daisy.

"Or ghosts," suggested Tom.

"Well, it's a mystery to me," said Dad, wiping cake mixture out of his ears.

He suddenly spotted Zingle. "What's that mop doing in here?" he asked.

"I'm not a mop," squeaked Zingle.

"It's not a mop," Tom squeaked quickly. "It's a cat."

"It doesn't look like a cat," said Dad.

"Hee-haw!" went Zingle.

"And it doesn't sound like a cat," said Dad.

"You're meant to go miaow," whispered Zack.

"Miaow!" squeaked Zingle.

"She's a very rare breed," said Daisy quickly. "She's a blue mop-haired cat."

"And she needs a home," said Zack. "Can she stay here?"

"No," said Zack's dad. "She'd get under Gran's feet."

Zingle jumped onto Gran's lap.

"Who's a fluffy-wuffy little kitty?" said Gran, stroking Zingle's fur. A very loud noise rumbled up and down the hall.

"What's that?" asked Dad.

"Thunder," said Zack.

"A drill," said Daisy.

"Stampeding dinosaurs," said Tom.

"Don't be silly," said Gran happily. "It's the cat. She's purring."

"Doesn't sound like purring," said Dad.

"It sounds just fine to me," said Gran. "I want to keep her."

"All right, then," said Dad. "What are you going to call her?"

"Zingle!" said Tom, Zack and Daisy together.

"That's a lovely name," said Gran. "Zingle it is."

"Hee-haw!" squeaked Zingle. "I mean miaow."

"Funny little cat," said Gran, scratching her between the antennae. "Now, is that cupcakes I can smell? I love cupcakes."

"Me too!" said Toppo, running in from the lounge.

Dad looked about in astonishment. "Who said that?"

Toppo hid.

"It was me," said Tom quickly. "I love cupcakes too."

"So do I," added Daisy.

"We all love cupcakes," said Zack.

"Then I'd better make another batch," said Dad, "so there's enough to go around."

"Cosmic!" yelled Tom.

REPORT

NAME

Zingle

EARTH IDENTITY

blue mop-haired cat

REPORT

Earthlings are very strange. They disguise themselves as walking cakes.

Earthling machines are very strange. They chase Earthlings. They blow Satniks out of windows. They whizz grandmothers up and down stairs.

It's very interesting.

Satniks Go Wild

Tom crept down his garden path. He was carrying a big bulging shopping bag.

"Why can't I walk on my lead?" said a voice from the shopping bag.

"Because Mum will stop us if she sees you, Fizz," said Tom. "We're going somewhere special, but dogs aren't allowed there."

"Is it school?" called Fizz. "Dogs aren't allowed in school."

"No, it's a lot better than school," said Tom.

"Then where is it?" asked Fizz.

"It's a surprise," said Tom.

"Zoops!" said Fizz. "I love surprises."

They came to Zack's house. Zack was waiting at the gate. Zingle was hiding in his hood.

"Where are we going, Earthlings?" she squeaked.

"It's a surprise," called Fizz.

"Zoops!" squeaked Zingle. "I love surprises."

"Good morning to you," came a cheerful voice and Toppo popped out of a hedge. "I was just putting a carrot in the pencil sharpener at school when my Satpad alarm pinged to remind me to come. Hope I'm not late."

"You're just in time," said Zack.

"Where are we going?" asked Toppo, jumping into the bag with Fizz.

"It's a surprise," called Fizz and Zingle together.

"Zoops!" said Toppo. "I love surprises."

They set off down the road.

"I can see Daisy!" squeaked Zingle in Zack's ear.

"She's standing by a sign," said Fizz, poking his trumpety nose out of the shopping bag.

"It says *The Really Wild Wildlife Park*," said Toppo, popping up beside him.

Daisy ran to meet them. She was wearing her green wellies with flowers on. She always wore them when she helped her dad muck out the elephants.

"Here's your surprise!" said Daisy. "A day at the wildlife park."

"So you can investigate the animals," added Tom.

"This will be even better than when we went to see the klapsquabblers back home!" yelled Fizz.

"Let's start investigating," said Toppo, climbing out of the bag.

"You must stay hidden," said Zack.

"But we're pretending to be Earth pets," said Toppo, "and we're getting very good at it."

"Hee-haw!" squeaked Zingle. "I mean, miaow. Everyone will think I'm a cat."

"Earth pets aren't allowed in The Really Wild Wildlife Park," explained Daisy.

"What about class rabbits?" asked Toppo.

"They're pets too," Daisy told him.

"We could disguise ourselves as Earthlings," said Fizz.

"That would be cosmic!" said Tom.

"It would *not* be cosmic," said Daisy firmly. "Someone might spot them and catch them."

"You're right," said Tom. "That would be awful."

"But you can come out when there's no one else around," said Zack.

"Follow me," said Daisy. "We'll go to Elephant Kingdom first."

"Zoops!" said Fizz. "I can't wait to investigate the elephants."

Daisy led them to the elephant enclosure. The elephants were in a huge field on the other side of a wall.

"There's no one here," she said. "It's safe to come out."

The Satniks jumped onto the wall.

"*They're* not elephants, silly Earthling," giggled Zingle. "They haven't got their shells on their backs."

"And they're not slithering about," added Fizz.

"Elephants don't slither," said Tom.

"And they don't have shells on their backs," put in Zack.

"Of course they do," said Toppo. "Look."

Ping!

His Satpad flew out of his ear. He tapped the keys with his claw and an image shimmered in the air.

"That's a snail," said Zack.

"Not an elephant?" asked Toppo.

"No," said Tom. "It's definitely a snail."

"Your Satpads are getting their animals in a muddle as usual," laughed Daisy.

"Looks like the sprungles are still flobbered," said Fizz.

"Here comes my dad," said Daisy. "You'd better hide again."

The three Satniks dived back into their hiding places.

"Hello there, Tom and Zack," said Daisy's dad. "Daisy told me you were coming. I expect you'd like to meet our Meg."

"Cosmic!" said Tom and Zack.

Daisy's dad took them to a big building next to the enclosure. It had a heavy door.

"What's a Meg?" whispered Zingle.

"Is it like a mug?" whispered Toppo.

"I thought we were going to meet the elephants," whispered Fizz.

"Here's Meg in her playhouse," said Dad, pushing open the door. "She knows Daisy, so you can all go in and see her. I'll be back later."

Daisy took them into a big room full of toys and ropes.

Meg was splashing happily around in a paddling pool.

The Satniks bounced out of their hiding places.

"A Meg *is* an elephant!" exclaimed Fizz.

"But why is it so small?" squeaked Zingle.

"Is it because of the water?" asked Toppo. "Water makes lots of things shrink."

"Yes! Water must make elephants shrink too!" said Fizz.

"No, it doesn't," laughed Daisy. "Meg is a *baby* elephant. She'll grow as big as the others."

The three Satniks peered closely at Meg.

"What are you doing?" asked Tom.

"We're waiting for Meg to grow, silly Earthling," squeaked Zingle.

Toppo tapped the keys on his Satpad. "How about a Top Toppo Trick while we wait?" He waved the Satpad at one of the buckets of water.

It rose in the air.

It began to tip over.

Splash!

Everyone jumped out of the way.
Meg gave a happy trumpeting call.

Whoosh!

A jet of water from Meg's trunk knocked
Toppo off his feet.

"Zoops!" he cried. "That was a Mega
Meg Trick!"

Meg curled her trunk around Fizz and
lifted him onto her back. He slid down
her trunk into the paddling pool.

"Double zoops!" he yelled. "This is fun!"

"My turn," said Toppo. He waved his
Satpad over his head and floated up to
Meg's back. Meg aimed her trunk at him
and shot him high into the air on her
waterspout.

"Your turn, Zingle," called Tom. "Come and join in." He looked around. There was no sign of her. "Where's Zingle?" he asked.

"I expect she's hiding," said Daisy. "Remember, she doesn't like getting her fur wet."

"Oh, dear," said Zack, "we have to find her before someone else does."

They searched Meg's playhouse. Tom stuck his head in the buckets and peered

under the paddling pool. Zingle was
nowhere to be seen.

"She must have run away!" said Daisy.

"Don't worry," said Fizz. "I'll use my
super Satpower to find her."

He twisted his ear.

Ping!

His Satpad landed on his hand. He
poked the keys with his nose.

Bleep . . . bleep . . . bleep went the
Satpad.

Fizz and Toppo jumped
into Tom's shopping bag.

"Follow the bleeps!"
called Fizz.

Tom, Zack and
Daisy burst out of Meg's
playhouse.

They ran past Monkey Mayhem. The
bleeps got louder.

They dashed around Wallaby Walk.
The bleeps got even louder.

They came to Lion Rock. A big lion with
a black mane was asleep near the fence.

BLEEEEEEP! went the Satpad.

Fizz jumped out of the shopping
bag and put his Satpad back in his
ear. "She's in there somewhere," he
announced, pointing towards the lion,
"with that grasshopper."

"That's not a grasshopper," said Zack. "Grasshoppers have six legs and they jump really high."

"Are you sure?" asked Fizz doubtfully.

"Positive," said Zack. "That's a lion."

"His name's Bernard," Daisy told them. "And he's very grumpy. The other lions don't go near him."

"He looks interesting," said Fizz eagerly. "We must investigate him when we've found Zingle."

Daisy was staring into the enclosure.

"That's funny," she said. "I don't remember Bernard having a blue fluffy toy."

"That's not a toy!" said Fizz. "That's Zingle. I told you she'd be here!"

Zingle was sitting in front of Bernard.

She waved happily at them. "Look at me, Earthlings," she called. "I've found a very interesting grasshopper."

"That's not a grasshopper," called Daisy, "and you must get out now!"

Bernard opened his mouth.

"I won't be long," squeaked Zingle. "I want to investigate these lovely teeth first."

"Zoops!" said Fizz. "They're very big."

"Yes, they are," said Zack.

"And they're very sharp," said Toppo.

"Yes, they are," said Tom.

"Let's go and investigate them too," said Fizz.

"No!" yelled Daisy.

It was too late. Fizz and Toppo had scrambled over the fence and scampered up to Bernard. Bernard's mouth opened wider.

"Get out of there!" yelled Daisy. "Bernard thinks you're food!"

"Silly Earthling," squeaked Zingle, peering into Bernard's mouth. "Satniks aren't food."

Bernard's mouth opened even wider.

"Quick, Toppo," called Zack. "Use your Satpower. Then you can all float up over Bernard's head."

"Great idea," said Toppo. "Bernard will love my Top Toppo Trick!"

Ping!

His Satpad appeared. He tapped some keys and waved it at his friends. The three Satniks floated up in the air.

Bernard gave a huge roar.

"Bernard's talking to us," said Zingle. "How sweet!"

"I'll make him float too," said Toppo. "He'll like that."

"No!" shouted Tom, Zack and Daisy.

It was too late. Toppo waved his Satpad at Bernard.

Bernard rose up in the air. He looked very surprised.

"Shall I send him over the fence?" called Toppo. "Then you can play with him too."

"NO!" shouted Tom, Zack and Daisy.

"Are you sure?" asked Toppo.

"Positive!" shouted Tom, Zack and Daisy.

Toppo waved his Satpad again. Bernard floated down to the ground.

So did the Satniks.

Bernard pounced on the Satniks.

The Satniks pounced on Bernard. Bernard looked very surprised.

"Look, Earthlings," squeaked Zingle. "We're playing a jumping game."

"Are you sure Bernard isn't a grasshopper?" called Fizz. "He can jump very high."

"He's definitely a lion," said Zack. "He's only got four legs."

The Satniks jumped up and down.

Bernard jumped up and down after them.

"I'm going to the penguins," said Daisy desperately. She dashed off.

"How can penguins help?" said Tom puzzled.

Daisy was soon back with a fishing net. It had a long handle. "Look, we can hook the Satniks out with this," she said.

"Great," said Zack. "I'll help."

Zack climbed onto Daisy's shoulders and poked the net over the fence.

"What fun!" said a squawky voice.
Tom whipped round.

A very peculiar creature was sitting on a
nearby bench. It looked like a parrot but it
had webbed feet, whiskers and a duck bill.

"You must be Tom," said the creature.
"Fizz told me all about you and your
friends. I'm Gronk."

"Cosmic!" said Tom. "Another Satnik.
Zack! Daisy! Come and meet Gronk."

"Hello, Gronk," panted Daisy as she
tottered past with Zack on her shoulders.

"Sorry, no time to chat," called Zack,
as he tried to catch the Satniks. "We're

rescuing your friends. They're in terrible danger."

"I don't think so," said Gronk. "They're just doing a spot of investigating."

Fizz, Toppo and Zingle jumped onto Bernard's rock. Gronk waved a wing at them.

"It's Gronk!" squeaked Zingle happily.

"What are you doing here, Gronk?" called Fizz.

"I'm investigating this pet shop, of course," said Gronk. "My Satpad told me to come. It said this is the place for buying pets and I'd like to buy that nice orange one." He pointed his wing at a giraffe that was looking over a wall. "Although I'll have to fold it up to get it into the spaceship."

"This isn't a pet shop," Tom told him. "It's a wildlife park. Your Satpad is getting its animal facts in a muddle. Its sprungles are flobbered."

"That must have happened when we nearly hit Mars," said Gronk.

Zack and Daisy fell in a heap. The net clattered to the ground beside them.

"It's no good," said Daisy. "The handle isn't long enough."

"And Bernard's going to eat the Satniks," said Zack.

"Satniks aren't food!" chuckled Gronk.

"But Bernard doesn't know that," explained Daisy. "He's a lion."

"Are you sure?" asked Gronk.

Bernard was prowling around the rock, licking his lips.

"Positive," said Daisy. "Can you help us?"

Gronk scratched his head with his wing. "I could use my super Satpower," he said.

"Cosmic," said Tom. "Does it turn your Satpad into a giant grabber?"

"Not exactly," said Gronk.

"A flying rescue machine?" asked Tom.

"Not really," said Gronk.

"Then what does it do?" demanded Zack.

"It makes noises," said Gronk.

"Will that help?" asked Daisy doubtfully.

"I promise it will," said Gronk. "I just have to get a bit closer to my friends."

He flapped his wings, took off and crashed into the fence.

"I meant to do that," he squawked as he slid to the ground. "I was testing the gravity."

He climbed up the fence using his duck bill and webbed feet. At last he reached the top.

"Made it," he said. "Now all I have to do is fly to the rescue."

He tripped on his wing, toppled into the enclosure and landed in a tree.

"I meant to do that," he squawked as he lost his balance and hung upside down from one foot.

"Come and join in, Gronk," called Toppo. "We're playing King of the Castle with Bernard."

"I can't," Gronk told them. "I promised the Earthlings I would rescue you."

"Silly Earthlings," squeaked Zingle. "We don't need rescuing."

"A promise is a promise," said Gronk solemnly.

He twiddled his whiskers with his wing. *Ping!*

A Satpad flew out of his feathers. He caught it with his spare foot and tapped the keys with his duck bill.

"I will send out the calming song of the lesser spotted dringpecker," he announced. "That will make Bernard very happy and he won't want to eat you."

A noise like an ambulance siren filled the air. Bernard's mane stood on end.

"Zoops!" said Gronk. "He doesn't like it. I'll try the soothing sound of the twittering twitwumble instead."

A dreadful screeching noise blasted out of the Satpad. Tom, Zack and Daisy put their fingers in their ears. Bernard put his paws over his ears.

"How strange," said Gronk. "He doesn't like that one either."

"Try something else," called Daisy.

Gronk tapped the keys again. "This is the night call of the sleepy satcrub," he told them.

A new noise echoed around the enclosure.

"That's terrible!" said Tom. "It sounds like a frying pan in a washing machine."

But Bernard rolled over and over, grunting happily.

"Now's your chance," Zack called to the Satniks. "You can escape."

The Satniks didn't move. They were staring at Bernard's claws.

"They're very big," said Fizz.

"Yes, they are," said Tom. "But . . ."

"And very sharp," said Toppo.

"They're cosmic!" said Tom. "But . . ."

"We won't be long, Earthlings,"

squeaked Zingle. "We're going to investigate Bernard's claws first."

"If you come now, we'll go to the ice-cream stand," called Daisy desperately.

"What's ice cream?" asked Fizz.

"It's a surprise," said Zack.

"Zoops!" said Toppo. "We love surprises."

He waved his Satpad at Fizz and Zingle. They all floated off Bernard's rock and over the fence.

"I'm coming too," squawked Gronk. "Watch me fly." He let go of the branch, flapped his wings wildly and plummeted.

"He forgot he was upside down," explained Fizz.

Gronk landed between Bernard's paws.

"I meant to do that," he squawked.

Bernard looked at Gronk. He opened his mouth very wide.

"He's going to eat him!" gasped Daisy.

To their surprise, Bernard gave Gronk a huge lick.

"That tickles," squawked Gronk. He rubbed Bernard's nose.

Bernard rumbled happily, closed his eyes and went to sleep.

"I'll come and see you tomorrow,"
Gronk whispered in Bernard's ear.
"I'll play you the sound of the warbling
wickertop. You'll like that one too."

He flapped his wings, took off, crashed
into a bouncy branch, pinged over the
fence and landed at Daisy's feet.

"I meant to do that," he squawked.

"Let's investigate ice cream now,"
said Toppo.

"Not so fast," said Gronk. "I must
pretend to be an Earth pet first. Fizz made
me a list. Fizz is good at lists."

He tapped the keys of his Satpad and
a list wobbled in the air.

"I haven't been to the pet shop, so I
don't know which pet to be," said Gronk.
"Can you help?"

Gronk's Important List, by Fizz

1. Do not let Earthlings know you're an alien.
2. Except for Tom, Zack and Daisy.
3. Do not pretend to be a dog or a rabbit or a cat.
4. Investigate the pet shop.
5. Decide which pet to be.
6. When you've decided, make a nest.

Daisy's dad came up, pushing a wheelbarrow full of dung.

"There you are!" he said. "I wondered where you'd all got to."

"Zoops!" whispered Fizz. "Hide, Satniks."

He jumped into the shopping bag.

Toppo and Zingle jumped in after him.

Gronk tried to jump in after them.
He got his foot tangled in his bill and
fell on top of Dad's boots.

"What's that?" gasped Dad.

"It's a parrot," said Zack.

"It's a duck," said Tom at the same time.

"I'm surprised you don't know, Dad,"
said Daisy. "It has parrot feathers, a duck
bill and cat's whiskers. It's a duck-billed
parrotpuss!"

"You know, like a duck-billed *platypus*,"
said Zack, "but a bit different."

"A duck-billed parrotpuss?" said Dad,
scratching his head. "Never heard of it."

"A duck-billed parrotpuss," said Daisy
firmly. "It's a very rare parrot."

"Then it must have escaped from the Bird World enclosure," said Dad. "I'll take it back."

"You can't," said Zack.

"He won't like it," said Tom.

"He's a baby," said Daisy.

"No, I'm not," squawked Gronk.

"He can talk!" said Dad in surprise.

"Of course I can," squawked Gronk.

"He *is* a parrot, after all," said Zack.

"His name's Gronk and he needs hand-rearing," said Daisy firmly. "I've decided to do that at home, Dad."

"All right then," said Dad. "At least he's not an elephant, like last time!"

He trundled his wheelbarrow away.

"Time for the ice cream," said Tom.

"Not so fast!" said Gronk. "I need to practise being a parrot first. I'll grow some fins and find a nice tank of water."

"That's a goldfish," Daisy told him.

"I knew that," said Gronk. "I meant I'll grow a curly tail and find a nice sty."

"That's a pig," said Zack. "Don't forget, your Satpad's sprungles are flobbered."

"I knew that," said Gronk. "So how am I going to find out about being a parrot?"

"That's easy," said Zack. "Parrots squawk."

"And they talk," said Daisy.

"And they sit on pirates' shoulders," said Tom.

"I don't know any pirates," said Gronk.

"That's OK," said Tom. "Parrots sit on other people's shoulders as well."

"I knew that," said Gronk. He flapped up onto Daisy's shoulder. "Time for the ice cream," he said.

"Is the ice cream fierce?" asked Fizz.

"Does it have spots?" squeaked Zingle.

"Is it furry?" asked Toppo.

"Ice cream isn't an animal," laughed Daisy. "It's Earthling food."

"And it tastes out of this world," said Tom.

A man walked by holding a cone piled high with three scoops of ice cream.

"That's an ice cream," said Zack, pointing.

In a flash, a long pink tongue shot out from Gronk's bill. It curled around the ice cream and whipped it off the cone.

"Zoops!" Gronk squawked, licking his bill. "It *does* taste out of this world."

"That's amazing!" said Tom. "I wish I could do that."

Gronk flapped off Daisy's shoulder and began to creep after a woman with a double chocolate cornet.

"What are you doing, Gronk?" asked Tom.

"I'm getting an ice cream for my friend Bernard," said Gronk.

"Lions don't eat ice cream," said Zack.

"Are you sure?" said Gronk.

"Positive," said Daisy. "Anyway, you mustn't pinch other people's ice creams. We'll buy you one each."

"We'll have the biggest ones in the wildlife park," said Zack.

"The biggest ones on Earth," cried Fizz.

"The biggest ones in the universe!" squawked Gronk.

"Cosmic!" yelled Tom.

REPORT

NAME

Gronk

EARTH IDENTITY

duck-billed parrotpuss

REPORT

Earthlings are strange. They think that lions eat Satniks. This is very silly as Satniks are not food.

Lions are strange. They don't eat ice cream even though ice cream is food. This is very silly as ice cream tastes out of this wrold . . . I mean . . . wordl . . . I mean . . . world.

P. S. I meant to do that.

PETS FROM SPACE

Collect all the PETS FROM SPACE *books*